MOG AT THE ZOO

for Emms

MOG at the ZOO

by Helen Nicoll
and Jan Pieńkowski

PUFFIN BOOKS

Meg, Mog and Owl went to the zoo

He flew past the flamingos

He zipped past the zebras

The crocodiles gave him a cheer

GO! GO! GO!

He turned
to talk
to
the
tigers

and
ran
slap
into
a tree

They put Mog in a cage and went

away to look him up in a book

Swop-swop
To-and-fro
Chop-chop
Let Mog go

Meg flew to the rescue
with one of her spells

An elephant gave her a bun

The
animals
went
to sleep

Pandemonium broke out

CHATTER

SQUAWK

ROAR

HOWL

HONK

..Squeak

GRRUNT

Whoo?

Meeow?

RATTLE

HISS GROAK

They had
breakfast
in a
tree

Goodbye!